THESEUS, MONSTER-KILLER

Also available from Hodder Children's Books
by Tony Robinson and Richard Curtis

Odysseus, Superhero
Odysseus Goes Through Hell

Theseus, Monster-killer

Tony Robinson and Richard Curtis
Illustrated by Chris Smedley

Hodder
Children's
Books

a division of Hodder Headline plc

From Tony to Kate and Huw Illingworth, and in memory of Dave.

From Richard to the Bad Girl in Black.

1

A Snake in the Sandal

It was night, a pitch black night. The sky was blacker than the blackest thing you've ever seen – and then a little blacker than that. The streets were full of deep, dark shadows. Everything was still. Then one shadow moved: it was a woman, dodging from doorway to doorway in the dark, with a small bundle in her arms. She was very old, bent double from fear and exhaustion, and she was crying. Suddenly, at the end of the street, three men appeared. Their swords were out. They were looking for her and ready for the kill. The woman flattened herself against a door and held her breath, terrified that she would be found. And then found dead the next morning. The men's echoing footsteps grew louder and louder. Had they seen her?

'I'm sure she went this way,' snapped the tall one.

'No, we've missed her,' growled the short one angrily.

'Let's try by the harbour,' added the one who was a

pretty normal size, but had very
bad teeth.

They moved off and the old
woman took her chance. She
staggered round the corner and
before her saw the looming
outline of the Palace of the
King of Athens. Holding
tight to her bundle, she
climbed the huge, high

steps and prayed that when she reached the massive
door at the top, someone would hear her knocking. And
they did. The great brass doors opened and she found
herself in an enormous dark room. Ghostly shadows
seemed to move in its corners, like animals moving in a
forest at night. But fear made the old woman bold, and
she shouted into the darkness:

'The King, the King! I must talk to the King! Bring me
to King Aegeus!!!'

In an instant the room was filled with the light of a
hundred flickering lanterns. The shadows turned into
people, and all their eyes were on the old woman
whose shoulder was cut and dripped blood on to the
stone floor.

Another second passed, then the giant doors at the
other end of the room crashed open, and there stood
the King: he was short and stocky and the bronze crown
on his head shone in the firelight.

'Who wants me?' he called.

The old woman stepped forward. Her voice choked as she spoke.

'My Lord – my King! Your summer palace has been attacked by soldiers. The Queen is dead. Everyone is dead!'

The King's face showed not a flicker of emotion. 'Everyone?' he asked quietly.

'Everyone except . . .' The old lady reached forward to show him what she held in her arms. It was a baby boy. 'Everyone except your son, Theseus.'

King Aegeus gently placed his hand on the old woman's shoulder and whispered, 'My brother Laius has done this.'

Then he wiped the blood from his hand, took his son in his arms and walked back through the towering doors. The whole palace waited to hear the sound of his rage and fury but there was silence – absolute silence. It was only later, just before morning, that the guard outside the King's room heard him crying.

When his wife was buried, Aegeus proclaimed that his son, baby Theseus, was to be taken to the town of Troezen.

'He will be safe there from my brother until he has grown to be a man. And when he is a man, then he will return home and together we will avenge his mother's death.'

'But no road in the world is as dangerous as the road to Troezen,' cried the old nurse. 'It's full of bandits and ogres and man-eating monsters so disgusting it makes your hair turn white just thinking about them.'

Aegeus gave a flicker of a smile. 'I won't be taking any risks with the life of the next King of Athens,' he replied. 'My son and I will go by sea.'

So they sailed safely to Troezen: but when they arrived, the King didn't go straight into the city. Instead, he took his six strongest soldiers to a nearby hill on the top of which sat an enormous stone.

'No man has ever lifted this stone,' he said. The soldiers weren't surprised. It was massive. Then King Aegeus added, 'You lot will be the first.'

And so the poor soldiers took off their helmets, rolled up their sleeves and got down to work. They heaved, they strained, they made funny little groaning noises. Their veins stood out on their foreheads like big blue worms and their muscles bulged like coconuts. And finally, *fffffiiiiinally*, the stone moved. But it didn't go shooting up above their heads – in fact, it didn't even reach their knees. No – all these tough guys could manage was a gap the size of a thimble between the stone

10

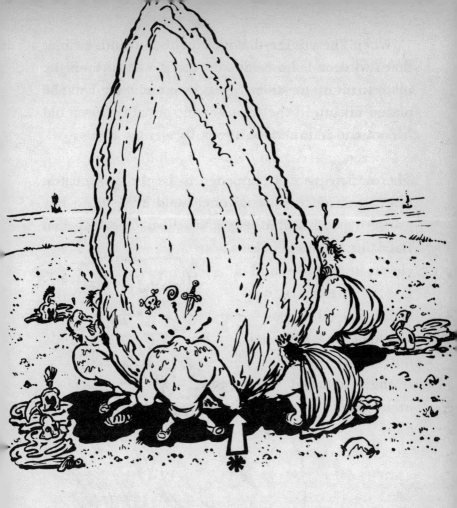

and the earth. Immediately Aegeus slipped a sword and a pair of sandals beneath it before DOOOMMMPH!!, the rock crashed down again and the men collapsed in an exhausted sweaty heap.

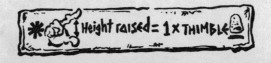

Height raised = 1 x THIMBLE

'When Theseus lifts that rock on his own and retrieves that sword and those sandals, that's when he will be ready to return to Athens,' Aegeus announced. Then he placed his son in the trust of two specially chosen old friends and returned to Athens. By sea.

The old friends just happened to be the two greatest teachers in Greece. If anyone could bring up a boy worthy to be King of Athens, it was them. One was called Daedalus: he was tall, thin, clever, shortsighted and the greatest inventor in the world. The other was Hercules: he was also tall, but strong, the strongest man in the world.

And the fastest runner. And the best fighter. Daedalus was going to teach Theseus to be clever. Hercules would teach him to be . . . a Hero.

For the next ten years, the pattern was the same. Every day Hercules raced Theseus up the hill and round the big stone, and every day Theseus ran a little faster.

And in the evening, Daedalus taught him maths.

Every day Hercules challenged Theseus to tear up trees and wrestle with snakes, and every day Theseus got a little stronger.

And in the evening, Daedalus taught him geometry.

Every day Hercules and Theseus banged their heads against the city walls, threw javelins at eagles, and fooled around with lions, and every day Theseus grew a little wilder.

And in the evening, Daedalus made Theseus work out difficult problems like: 'How *do* you calculate the amount of water in a bath?'

And in the end, Theseus had had enough of the man in glasses.

'Look,' he said one night, throwing his exercise book firmly in the dustbin. 'I'm not interested in maths, I'm not interested in geometry and I'm definitely not interested in the amount of water in a bath, or for that matter in a shower or a wash-basin. All this brain-box stuff is a waste of your time and a waste of mine. Please will you go away.'

Daedalus was silent. His pupil might be cocky, he might be rude, but he was the King's son and Daedalus cared what happened to him. He was going to have to learn that strength without brains was like a horse without legs – useless.

'Go away,' Theseus repeated firmly.

'Very well,' said Daedalus, sadly. 'You're the Prince – I'm only the teacher. I pray that you will learn by yourself the importance of brains, and that you won't pay too heavily for this mistake.' Then he packed his inventions – his pen that wrote underwater, his self-tying shoelaces and his luminous book for reading after dark – and left the city.

'That's the last I'll see of Theseus,' he thought as he trudged off into the sunset. Which just goes to show how wrong even the cleverest bloke can be.

So now Theseus spent all his time with Hercules, and he grew stronger and stronger until one day, the day of his fifteenth birthday, he woke up, looked out of the window at the big stone on the hill-top and knew, just *knew* that he could lift it. He strode out of the town and someone shouted at him, 'Theseus, where are you going?' But the young Prince didn't answer. He just kept on walking until he came to the bottom of the hill.

'He's going to try and lift the big stone,' went up the cry. And everyone dropped their knitting and their tools and their toy soldiers and streamed out of the city to follow him. It was like the Pied Piper of Hamelin – in a second, *whoosh*, the city was empty, everyone running at the heels of Theseus, no one of course believing for a moment that he could lift the thing. 'It took six big men to lift it when the King was here, and that was only just,' said someone with a long memory.

'Still, it makes a day out,' agreed a couple who'd brought along some bread and cheese.

When they reached the stone, everyone gathered in a circle – peasants, soldiers, children, stray dogs, peanut sellers – and, in the centre, Theseus stripped down to the waist. He took a deep breath, and everyone went silent. Then he crouched, squeezed his fingers under the rock . . . 'I bet that hurt,' said one kid . . . and heaved. And *heaved*. And, inch by inch, the rock left the ground; at first it was toe high, then knee high, then waist high, and

finally right above his head. With one last explosive push, he threw it aside and it rolled down the hillside, flattening vines, olive trees and goats, until it flew over the white cliff and smashed into a thousand pieces on the beach below. Everyone screamed, and cheered, and threw their hats in the air, even the couple who hadn't noticed that, along with the vines and the goats, their bread and cheese had been fair and squarely squashed.

But Theseus didn't watch the stone as it rolled away. He was staring down at his feet. There, where the stone had been, was a short, stubby, rusty sword with a big chunky ruby in its handle and a pair of old leather sandals. A snake was sticking its head through the top of one of the sandals, and its eyes were shining with hunger. But a man who could throw a boulder wasn't going to be worried by a little snake, even though its poison sacs were bulging and its tongue was quivering in a distinctly threatening manner. No, Theseus just flicked it out of the way, and placed his feet firmly inside the shoes.

'I've done it,' he said. 'Now I'm going back to Athens.'

'But there's no ship ready,' Hercules pointed out.

'Ship, my foot! I'm going by land.'

Everyone gasped – 'What about the bandits, what about the ogres, what about the . . .' and their hair began to turn white as they thought about it. But Theseus just smiled, picked up the sword and

17

left Troezen forever. As far as he could see, he wasn't worthy to be Prince of Athens if he couldn't deal with a slightly tricky journey.

After ten days, he saw a village ahead of him, and beyond it a great forest growing up the sides of a mountain. He strode briskly towards it, when suddenly villagers in big green hats came running up to him crying, 'Whatever you do, don't enter the forest!'

'Why not?' asked Theseus, not breaking his stride for a moment.

'Because you'll fall into the clutches of the Great Tosser,' they shouted, every one of them shivering with fear.

'Oh, yeah – and what's his game?' asked Theseus, heading on.

'He tosses people off mountains,' they replied, but already Theseus was too far away to hear. He strode on into the forest, unafraid.

The sky above him grew darker and the air around him grew colder. The path wound higher and higher.

On Theseus' left side the huge
trees rustled with unseen
creatures. On his right
was the mountainside,
rocky, sheer and
dizzyingly frightening.

Then something burst out of the trees. It was a little
man the height of a small umbrella stand.

'Prepare for combat,' said the little man, standing still
and perfectly balanced, ready to attack. 'One of us must
die.'

'Fair enough,' said Theseus and with a deft left-footer
kicked the little man off the mountain. 'It's you.'

Higher and higher Theseus climbed until suddenly
two enormous trees blocked his path.

What a bore, he thought. But then he looked down,
and noticed something very strange. The trees were
wearing sandals. In fact, they weren't trees at all. They
were legs; and perched on top of them was a huge
body, and on top of the body Theseus assumed there
must be a massive head because, from somewhere up in
the clouds, a voice came bellowing down to him.

'Turn back, stranger,' it went. 'I am the Great Tosser.'

'I thought the Great Tosser was the little bloke back
there,' replied Theseus.

'No,' boomed the bellowing voice. 'That was my
cousin – the Little Tosser. He was just on a training
scheme. Now prepare for combat, one of us must die.'

'Fair enough,' said Theseus for the second time that day. But this time he wasn't very happy about it. How could he possibly win a fight against something the size of a small castle?

Then his mind flashed back to long ago – all those boring old chess games he'd been forced to play with boring old Daedalus. And what was it Daedalus kept telling him?

Always go for your opponent's weak spot.

And as he remembered, he glanced down at the Tosser's right sandal. He could see the giant's little toe sticking out, all fat and pink and hairy, and it wiggled every time the Tosser spoke.

Theseus immediately dropped to the ground, seized the toe in both hands and yanked it backwards.

CRAAAAAAACK!!!!! went the toe,
the Tosser jack-knifed with pain,
and as his great red face
loomed into sight to inspect
the damage, Theseus leapt
into the air and nutted him
on the nose.

'WHAAAAARGHH!!' went
the Tosser as he rocked
backwards on his heels. Round
and round went his arms
like two giant windmills as he
desperately tried to regain

his balance. But he was too big and heavy and clumsy. He snatched at a branch – it came away in his hands. He grabbed at a tree – and pulled it up by its roots. Then slowly, so slowly it seemed like slow motion, the Great Tosser toppled backwards off the path and fell down!

down!

down!

the mountainside and crashed on to the rocks below. He lay there dead as a dodo – and that's very dead indeed.

Night came, and Theseus just kept on walking. Early the following morning he came to a clearing dotted with toadstools and little clumps of pine trees.

A friendly old peasant in a red hat popped out from behind a tree. 'Whatever you do, don't go any further,' he urged, 'Or you'll fall into the clutches of Pine Bender.'

'Really?' said Theseus.

'Yes, really,' replied the old man. 'He drugs travellers with mysterious potions and when they're asleep, he bends the topmost branches of two pine trees down to the ground, and ties their arms and legs to them. Then he lets go, the pine trees shoot up into the air, the travellers are ripped up the middle and their mangled bodies are left dangling from the tree tops.'

'Thanks for the warning,' murmured Theseus, turning slightly green.

'You look a bit shaken, son,' said the friendly peasant. 'Why not sit down with me for a minute and have a flask of Dandelion and Burdock.'

Gratefully, Theseus took the flask, tilted his head back and poured a stream of the refreshing liquid into his mouth.

He gazed up. What a glorious forest it was! The pine

trees grew hundreds of feet into the air and their tops were covered with beautiful red flowers. Beautiful blood red flowers.

Wait a minute! Pine trees have funny little pine cones, thought Theseus. *Not beautiful blood red flowers.* These weren't flowers at all!!! They were the left over bits from the bodies of poor unfortunate travellers.

SPLOOODGE! Theseus spat the poisoned Dandelion and Burdock straight into the friendly peasant's face and ripped off his red hat. But it wasn't only the hat that came off. As Theseus pulled the hat, the peasant's whole face seemed to come away in his hand as well.

Because it wasn't a face at all, but a Friendly Peasant Mask, underneath which lurked his drinking companion's real features. And they were horrible features. Instead of pleasant blue eyes, Theseus saw vicious yellow eyes, black teeth and slaver dribbling down the monster's chin.

'*You* are Pine Bender,' said Theseus, his eyes shining with anger.

'Yes,' squawked Pine Bender and dark brown spittle shot from his mouth as he rushed towards Theseus, his hands like vulture's claws about to rip the flesh off their victim. But Theseus was too quick for him, and in a second had him tight under one arm. Then, as Pine Bender kicked and wriggled and whined, Theseus pulled down two pine trees with his free hand and tied the struggling murderer to the topmost branches.

'This is the last time you'll have anything to do with people being torn to bits,' he said, and let go of the branches.

Then he turned his back and went on his way. Behind him there was a dull ripping noise – like the sound of a wet newspaper being torn in two. But Theseus just kept on walking.

On the twentieth morning he reached the other side of the mountain and ahead of him he could see the distant towers of the city of Athens. Soon he was surrounded by hundreds of excited peasants in different coloured hats.

'Theseus has killed the Pine Bender!' they cheered.

'Theseus has killed the Great Tosser!' they chanted.

'Theseus has killed the Great Tosser's cousin!' shouted one little bloke, but he was told to shut up. Then they lifted Theseus up in the air and carried him shoulder high across a great plain to the gates of the city. But as they did, Theseus wondered . . .

Who would welcome him home?

Who was in control of Athens?

His father – or his treacherous uncle Laius?

The gates swung open. Theseus took a deep breath and stepped inside.

'How good to see you after all this time, my son,' said a voice and a man appeared out of the shadows and hugged Theseus tight to his chest.

'News had already reached me that you were approaching the city, so I have prepared a banquet to celebrate your return – follow me.'

But he didn't take Theseus along the wide open streets towards the palace. Instead they threaded their way through tiny winding alleys which stank of rats and rotting refuse, until they came to a tiny door. The man looked furtively about him, then took a key from his inside pocket.

The door creaked open. Inside was a vast banqueting hall. There were waiters running hither and thither carrying plates piled high with steaming boars' heads, stuffed with black olives and pink cod's roe. There were tumblers tumbling, jugglers juggling and clowns making complete idiots of themselves. There was a twenty piece orchestra playing that week's number one – Athenian Rhapsody – and massive oak tables around which sat a hundred hungry soldiers who drummed their daggers on their plates as Theseus entered.

'Hail Theseus the Great!' they shouted. 'Let the celebration dinner begin!' And it sure did start – never has more food been stuffed down more mouths in a shorter length of time. And when the last boar's head had been chewed, Theseus' host quietened his guests and lifted a jewelled coronet high above Theseus' head.

'A present for my son Theseus,' he said and grinned gleefully from ear to ear.

And can you guess why he was so happy? Was it because his darling son had been returned to him after sixteen years?

No, it wasn't.

Was it because he was glad to see his hungry friends full of pig meat and cod's roe?

Not on your life.

The reason he was so happy was because this man wasn't Theseus' father at all. He was his uncle, Laius, the vile traitor who had already killed Theseus' mother. He was happy because he knew that inside the coronet he was holding was a row of tiny spikes covered with poison squeezed from the stomachs of funnel web spiders. Horrid spiders. Horrid poison. Horrid spikes. As he slowly lowered the coronet, he was smiling because he knew that in a few seconds Theseus would be dead. Theseus was smiling too – but that was because he had no idea that a hideously horrible death was only two inches away.

BLAAMM!! The door burst open and there stood King Aegeus with his army behind him. His eyes flashed

round the room. He saw the deadly coronet, he saw his brother's face turning from triumph to terror, he saw the young man at the banqueting table, and in front of the young man he saw a short stubby sword with a ruby in its handle and an old pair of sandals. And he recognised them.

Without a word, Aegeus drew his knife and threw it like a supersonic silver dart across the hall.

STOOOOOOMP!! Laius screeched with pain as his hand was pinned to the wall. The coronet went spinning across the room and rolled to a standstill in the middle of the marble floor. There was a hissing noise, and dark, choking smoke gushed out as the poison dripped from its spikes and turned the floor black.

Whatever it was in that coronet, Theseus now knew it hadn't been mild shampoo.

Then Aegeus turned to Theseus. 'Welcome home, son,' he said, and they both smiled and then hugged each other. They hardly noticed or cared as Laius slipped whimpering out of the room, leaving one of his fingers behind on the wall.

2
The Smell of
Rotten Meat

The path seemed safe enough.

Aegeus nodded his men forward and a thousand Athenian soldiers marched confidently into the valley.

Two years had gone by since Theseus had returned home – two years of peace and prosperity for Athens. But always in the background hung the dark threat of Four-Fingered Laius, Aegeus' evil brother. The King knew he must seek and destroy him before he brought the country to its knees with his bunch of ruthless guerrilla fighters.

And now Aegeus looked anxiously at the mountains on either side. There was absolute silence except for the Crunch! Crunch! Crunch! of his soldiers' boots.

Then, from a bank of ferns high above him, a partridge broke cover. The King glanced round; something must have disturbed it. He caught a glimpse of something shiny reflected by the sun. Then it was gone.

What was it? He smiled wryly to himself. He knew only too well.

'Back! Back! Back!' he shouted. 'It's an ambush!' But it was too late. With a terrifying roar the camouflaged soldiers of his treacherous brother Laius rose up from the mountain slopes and a hail of javelins and arrows rained down on the Athenians.

Immediately Aegeus' men formed themselves into the shape of a giant tortoise, covering themselves and their comrades with their shields, leaving only tiny slits through which their archers could fire back. But slowly and methodically their enemies moved down the mountain towards them. Any minute now they would be overwhelmed. A rather nasty massacre was just around the corner. The Athenian tortoise was about to be crushed.

But then, high in the mountains, a trumpet rang out. Then another. Then another. The ambushers swished round in fear to see where the sound was coming from. They had an awful feeling that the people playing trumpets weren't members of a jazz band. And they were right. Galloping towards them were five hundred hand-picked Athenian horsemen, and at their head was a young boy on a white charger. It was Prince Theseus, furiously waving a short chunky sword around his head – a sword with a ruby in its handle.

Aegeus' army cheered, stopped acting like a tortoise and charged their attackers. And, of course, there was nowhere for evil Laius' guerrillas to run to. They were sandwiched between Theseus' horsemen and his father's foot soldiers and it was definitely the nastiest sandwich they'd ever tasted.

The battle was short and bloody. The cowardly Laius and a few of his nobles sneaked away right at the beginning, but the rest of his army soon lay dead on the battlefield. It would be a long time before they'd cause trouble again.

Aegeus and Theseus stood silently watching the last few guerrillas being dragged away, then turned and playfully slapped each others' hands.

'Congratulations,' said Aegeus. 'Your plan worked. Let the celebrations begin. Pull out the large banqueting tables. Summon forth the amusing clowns with big red noses. Tune the big guitars for a lusty sing-song and let's get so drunk we have to get dragged home by our hair.'

But when they arrived back in Athens, there were no celebrations: no crowds, no banquets, no massive barrels of second-rate grog. Everywhere was completely deserted except for a small group of women dressed in black, standing by the city gates, wailing and rubbing black ashes into their faces. Aegeus leapt off his horse and rushed up to them.

'What's happening?' he bellowed. 'We've just won a great victory – what possible reason is there for you to stand howling here like mourners weeping for the dead. Come on! Lighten up!'

'The men from Minos' are here,' came the quiet whisper of a reply.

Aegeus' face went grey. Then, almost absent-mindedly, he wiped a tear from the cheek of one of the women and walked on towards the palace leading his horse in silence.

'Who's Minos?' asked Theseus, trotting behind.

His father sighed before he replied, 'Minos is King of Crete, which is the most powerful state in Greece. Every nine years, to keep out of trouble, Athens has to send him seven caskets of gold, seven young men, and seven young women. The gold goes to King Minos himself. The young men and women go to the Minotaur.'

'The what?'

Aegeus grasped Theseus by the shoulders and looked deep into his eyes as he explained the horror. Theseus had never seen his father look frightened before.

'Somewhere below the Palace of King Minos lives a monster called the Minotaur. It is half a giant man, and half a giant bull, with dark green scaly skin and broken teeth stained red with human blood. Every year, Minos sacrifices fourteen young Greeks to it. He sends them into his maze, which is so brilliantly designed – God knows by whose sick mind – so full of twists and turns that it's impossible for anyone to find their way out. But the Minotaur knows every inch of it. The young men and women who enter it never come out – the monster eats them alive.'

'And *this* year, it's Athens' turn to provide a meal for the Minotaur, is it?' asked Theseus.

'That's right,' replied Aegeus. 'Tonight, in the temple, the young people will draw lots to decide who should go.'

'Well, I'll go for one,' said Theseus, 'and try and sort this thing out.'

But Aegeus tightened his grip like a vice on the shoulders of his only son.

'No. You are the King's son. The next King of Athens. You must stay.'

That night the entire population crowded into the temple to witness the choosing of the fourteen victims. At the altar the priests set up two enormous pots, one made of jade and the other of onyx. And each pot was full of stones – one for each boy and girl in the city.

A gong sounded and a long queue of Athenian girls shuffled up to the jade pot, dipped their hands in and pulled out a stone. If they picked a white one they were safe, if it was black they were doomed. Soon the temple was ringing with cries of relief and cries of terror, and seven young girls knew they were going to die.

Then it was the boys' turn. One after another they approached the onyx pot and the shouts and cries rang out again. But when six boys had drawn out the cursed black stones, there was a commotion at the back of the crowd. Someone was pushing his way through.

'It's Prince Theseus,' hissed an old woman, and the crowd pulled back to let him pass. He strode up to the altar, drew his sword and brought it down hard on the onyx pot. The pot smashed into pieces, scattering the pebbles across the temple floor. Then the Prince bent down, picked up the remaining black pebble and put it in his pocket.

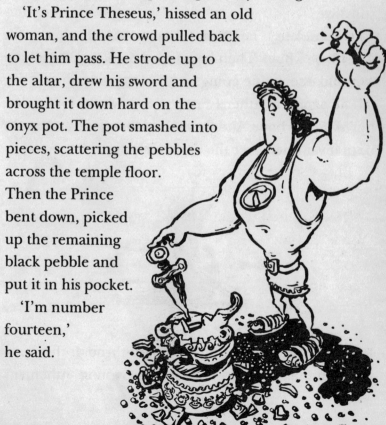

'I'm number fourteen,' he said.

Next morning the fourteen young Athenians were led out of the city and down to the harbour. The Cretan ship was waiting for them; blood red, with an enormous carved bull's head on the bow, and huge jet black sails.

Aegeus looked at his son, his face a mixture of pride and sadness. Theseus threw his big arms round his father.

'I'll come back,' he said. 'We all will.'

'If you return safely,' replied Aegeus, 'lower those hideous black sails as you enter the harbour, and hoist white ones in their place. Then I'll know you are still alive.'

'Okeedokee,' laughed Theseus. 'And cheer up. They'll be white.' Then he jumped on board, for all the world like someone going on a holiday cruise.

The people of Athens watched as slowly the boat sailed out of the harbour. And they stayed there, still and silent, until it vanished over the dark horizon.

For days, the blood red ship sailed through the open sea, until early one morning the young Athenians heard an eerie drumming sound. They raced up on deck and saw ahead of them the land of Crete. It was not what they expected of a great city. The beach was littered with rotting vegetables and dead sea birds, the hillsides were covered with squalid shacks. Beggars and skinny dogs picked their way through the muddy streets. But the worst thing was the smell, like an open sewer.

Yet in the middle of this city of slums was a massive magnificent grey palace. Clearly one man had all the money and all the power and he wasn't sharing it. And clearly he was a nasty piece of work.

As the boat drew nearer the drumming grew louder and louder until it was so deafening that the Athenians had to cover their ears. Then the boat stopped and the drums went quiet. Lined up on the sand was a long procession of musicians and from their ranks stepped fourteen young women who climbed aboard and placed a garland round the neck of each Athenian in turn.

The last to receive one was Theseus. A short dark Minoan girl with serious eyes said, 'Welcome. I am Ariadne, daughter of King Minos.'

Theseus said nothing. He merely ripped off the garland and angrily threw it in the sea. He wasn't having anything to do with all this pomp and ceremony. 'As I see it,' he said, 'me and my friends are about to be murdered and that's that. This is no time for flowers and dignified speeches.'

Then the drumming began again and the long procession, with the Athenians in the middle, wound its way up to the palace. There was a small iron grille in the palace wall. As they approached, it swung open and the Athenians were stripped of their weapons and flung inside. Then the gate swung shut again. Ahead of them was a dark tunnel with a blaze of light at the end of it. Cautiously they walked onwards until they burst out into the open again and a huge roar filled the air.

They were in the middle of an enormous arena, like clowns in a circus, and all around them on stone seats

were thousands of Minoans, laughing and cheering
and clapping. For the Minoans this was clearly party
time – there were souvenir Minotaur mugs, Minotaur
hats with little wooden horns, and the ice-cream sellers
were doing fast business with their Minotaur Special –
vanilla with two chocolate flakes, one for each horn.

Theseus stood calmly in the middle and stared haughtily around. Up on a high throne in the middle of the crowd, he could see a burly man with long black hair, wearing a crown made out of bulls' horns. That must be Minos – but who was that next to him?

Theseus couldn't believe his eyes.

There, beside the King, stood his old school master, Daedalus, the teacher who was so brainy and so boring that Theseus had sent him packing!

And at that moment, Daedalus himself caught Theseus' eye. But he didn't jump with shock, or anything like that. Instead, slowly and imperceptibly, he just shook his head. Theseus guessed immediately that it was a sign that he should pretend not to know him, and so he looked quickly away.

By now a procession of young Minoan women, led by Princess Ariadne, were handing out exotic food and drink to the Athenians. Ariadne presented Theseus with a gold plate on which wobbled a grey green jelly with a dead fish in the middle of it.

'Accept this exquisite Minoan delicacy,' she said in a loud voice, and then softly whispered, 'Stay awake tonight. Someone wants to see you. I'll take you to him.'

That night Theseus lay in his cell waiting and vaguely considered that he might die tomorrow. It didn't bother him too much. *You've got to go some time*, he thought, *and back home I might have been run over by a municipal donkey and cart.* But at that moment, slowly and quietly the door opened and there stood Ariadne. 'Follow me,' she said and they padded down long grey corridors lit by a few flickering torches.

Soon they were in Daedalus' room.

'When you were a child,' he said, 'you used to yawn in my lessons and look out of the window. There was always a comic hidden in your text books. You wouldn't listen when I told you that a Prince needs to develop his brain as well as his muscles. But it will take more than strength to get you out of the Great Maze – no one has ever paid a visit to the Minotaur and returned to tell the tale.' Theseus knew that Daedalus was right. For once in his life he listened to his lesson, and he listened hard.

'Take this ball of string with you. Then at the entrance, tie one end to the door and unwind it as you go in. That way you'll be able to find your way back again.'

'But how will he kill the Minotaur?' asked Ariadne anxiously. 'Its skin is tougher than the strongest metal in the world.'

'True – but it has one weakness,' replied Daedalus.

'And you should always go for your opponent's weak spot,' added Theseus.

Daedalus smiled ruefully. 'I'm glad you remember something I taught you,' he said. 'Yes – there's one thing that's strong enough to pierce the Minotaur's skin, and that's the horn on its head.'

'So I'll have to talk it into stabbing itself?' asked Theseus cheekily, just like when he was a boy.

'Something like that,' replied Daedalus. 'Work it out for yourself. If you succeed, Ariadne will show you how to escape from the palace. But you must take her with you. She's strong and clever and hates her father's kingdom. If it's discovered that she aided your escape, she'll be killed.'

'But what about you?' asked Theseus.

'I'll come if I can,' said Daedalus.

'But how come you're here in the first place?'

'I built the maze,' answered his old teacher, and bowed his head in shame.

Ariadne led Theseus back to his cell.

'Good luck tomorrow,' she said. 'Are you frightened?'

'No!' replied Theseus stoutly. '*Well* . . . a bit.'

'No need. You'll be all right,' said Ariadne and she kissed him.

After she'd gone, Theseus lay listening to the silence – a silence broken only by an occasional bull-like roar from somewhere deep under the palace.

At noon the cell doors swung open and the Athenians began their journey to the maze. They marched for miles down gloomy winding corridors. Cold and damp began to seep into their bodies as they plunged deeper and deeper into the bowels of the earth. The walls were rougher than the stubble on a giant's beard and tiny, slithery animals jumped on them and nipped at them as they passed, having a nibble before the Minotaur had his big meal. Then, at the end of a long flight of slippery steps covered with green slime, they saw ahead of them a gigantic carved bull's head with blazing torches for eyes, and a massive black studded door where its mouth should have been. The Minoan guards heaved the door open and the Athenians were roughly shoved inside. There was a slam, then a rattle of chains and the door was bolted behind them.

They were inside the maze. And if history was anything to go by, it was the door of their coffin that had just closed behind them.

It was pitch black, and they had to grope about to get their bearings.

'AAAARRGHHH!!!' Someone let out a terrified scream: he'd tripped over something. It was a skull – a human skull. One of the young men began to moan with terror.

43

'Oh, get a grip!' snapped Theseus sharply. 'Here. Do something useful. Tie this string to the door. I'm going exploring.' And with that, he began to inch his way through the maze, unrolling the ball of string as he went. The other Athenians just assumed he'd gone mad and waited for their death.

The walls were jagged and sharp, like enormous stone thorns; they tore at Theseus' clothes and ripped his hands. And now he could smell the foul stench he had noticed when they first arrived – a smell of sewage, and rotting meat and death – it was so strong his stomach churned and his eyes watered.

He started in fright as the blood-thirsty bull's roar resounded in his ears and echoed and re-echoed round every wall of the maze.

Then there was silence. Everything was quiet and still.

First Theseus waited. Then cautiously he turned a sharp corner. Ahead of him was something dark and enormous with blazing yellow eyes and hot breath. In the half light its shiny skin glistened like the skin of a toad – but it was twice the size of an elephant.

Theseus knew he was face to face with death itself.

But there was no time to be afraid – in a second there was a clatter of enormous hooves and the beast reared and charged at Theseus, slobbering and chuckling as it came. Theseus leapt and dodged out of its way. A moment's silence, then a crunch of stones as the monstrous bull turned and charged again. Again Theseus dodged, and this time the Minotaur's horns missed him by a cat's whisker – and a pretty skinny whisker at that. There was a screech of pebbles, and it charged yet again. Theseus made to jump, but instead, his foot slipped on something disgusting and wet. It might have been a kidney. The Prince of Athens fell defenceless on the floor.

The Minotaur seemed to know it had won. It let out a triumphant bellow and lowered its head to deliver the final thrust. But when it was almost on him, Theseus sprang up with a last burst of energy and vaulted astride the monster's head, riding it like a wild bull. He grasped one of its horns, and heaved and twisted. There was a terrible crunching sound, like a young tree being torn out of the earth by its roots.

Then . . .

ARRGGHH!!.....

Back at the entrance, the Athenians heard a terrible cry. A death cry. They waited in terror. Then they heard the sound of something coming towards them. It was breathing heavily. They clung to each other, knowing death was on its way. And then . . .

'Wow – I'm puffed!' said Theseus. 'Anyone want a ball of string?'

The Athenians were so stunned with relief, they couldn't speak.

'Oh, yes, and by the way – the Minotaur's dead,' added the young hero.

In triumph, the Athenians hurled themselves at the massive studded door. On the other side the guards tried to keep it shut, but they didn't stand a chance. BLAAAMMM!!!! The door burst its hinges and crashed to the ground. Beneath it lay the guards – squashed flat like armoured pancakes. The Athenians raced out – and there, in the shadows, stood Ariadne. 'You'll be wanting this,' she said, and threw Theseus his stubby sword and a big nervous smile. 'Now follow me.'

And, very much alive, they bounded up the green slimy stairs that only an hour before they had gone down to await their death. On they pressed through secret doors and tiny passages, killing any Minoan who got in their way, until, at last, in a tangle of plumbing, they came to a massive drain pipe. 'This is the way out,' said Ariadne. 'Nothing personal.'

One after another they climbed into it and slid down, down, down, until, with a mighty plop, they found themselves lying on the ground outside the palace walls.

But there was not a moment to rest. Above them they heard a roar: 'Stop the prisoners! Stop my daughter!' They looked over their shoulders and saw the outline of King Minos, his crown of bulls' horns glinting in the afternoon sun.

'Thanks for having us!!' the laughing Theseus shouted back, and sprinted down to the beach and on to the ship. With one blow of his sword, he cut the mooring rope free and swiftly the Athenians grabbed the oars and hoisted the black sails, bound for home.

BLAAM!

Behind them the city gates burst open and there was Daedalus racing towards the quayside pursued by hundreds of Minoan soldiers.

But his skinny pink legs just wouldn't carry him fast enough. The boat was already pulling out towards the open sea.

'Jump!!!!' shouted Theseus, while there was still a chance. 'Swim to the boat!!!!'

'I can't swim,' Daedalus shouted back, and a second later the soldiers had surrounded him. 'I never learnt how,' he muttered to himself as they led him away. 'No matter how clever you are, you're never quite clever enough.'

3
The Back Leg of an Ant

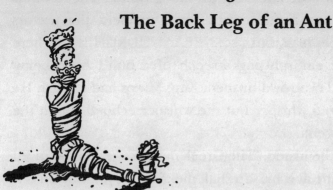

'Traitor! Traitor! Dirty Greek traitor!'

Daedalus lay bound and gagged in the middle of the giant arena, while all around him hundreds of angry Minoans stood on their seats chanting and waving their fists.

'You gave away the secret of the maze,' they yelled. 'Because of you the Minotaur is dead.'

Then someone spat at him, someone else threw a handful of rotten figs and yoghurt, and pretty soon a shower of filthy garbage was hailing down on him. A lump of cold baked beans hit him splat on the nose.

'Stop!' A young boy raced out of the crowd and stood in front of Daedalus shouting. 'Leave him alone! How dare you treat my father like this!'

'That's Icarus, the traitor's son,' shouted a weedy voice in the crowd. 'Kill him! Kill them both!'

And suddenly it wasn't garbage the crowd was hurling. It was coins and stones and bricks.

Icarus was knocked to the ground. The crowd's roar reached fever pitch. In a moment the traitors would be dead, but . . . NEEAAUUURGH!!! . . . there was the ear splitting screech of a bull's horn being blown. The crowd hushed. King Minos had arrived. He spoke in a whisper but the whisper echoed round the whole arena.

'Yes,' he hissed. 'The Greek maze maker has betrayed us, and he and his son shall die. But not yet. Daedalus is the most cunning craftsman known to man. First he shall make me a new Minotaur, a mechanical monster so powerful that no one will be able to resist it . . . not even Theseus.'

By now the Greeks were well out of Minoan waters. The bright summer sun was shining, smiling dolphins were leaping in and out of the sea, and everyone was getting nicely tanned. One bunch were playing quoits with the death garlands the Minoans had given them, a girl was being sick over the side – but she wasn't complaining, at least she was alive. Even the jet black sails looked a little less gloomy now.

Ahead of them lay the island of Naxos, shimmering in the sunlight. It was a magical island, covered with green forest skirted by little fringes of silver sand. Wisps of purple and crimson smoke appeared between the trees and the occasional sound of a flute echoed across the water, but no one appeared to watch the ship go by.

Ariadne was gazing in silence when Theseus interrupted her thoughts.

'We won't anchor here,' he said. 'I don't fancy being ambushed in those woods.'

Ariadne found it hard to imagine why anyone on Naxos would want to ambush them – she was sure there were better things to do on the island than bash people over the head – but she said nothing. She just sat and listened to the haunting strains of the unseen flute player in the woods.

'Not much longer now, and we'll be home,' Theseus went on, not noticing she was in a strange mood. 'My father'll be dead chuffed when I come sailing into the harbour and hoist a pair of white sails – and I can't wait to see his face when he sees I've got a wife! I wonder if he'll abdicate straight away.'

Still Ariadne didn't speak.

'Strictly between you and me, I'm dying to be in charge,' said Theseus, pressing on. 'When I'm King and you're Queen, we'll eliminate my uncle Laius, then you can stay at home and do the palace-work while I wipe out any countries that cause us trouble. Then we'll go back to Minos and take our revenge on your father.'

Slowly Ariadne turned to him. 'I've not escaped one tyrant just to marry another,' she said softly.

But Theseus wasn't listening. 'I mean, you've got to be practical, haven't you. If we don't flatten them, they'll flatten us, right?' he said confidently, then patted

53

Ariadne on the head and moved off towards the wheel house.

When suddenly . . .

Plop!

There was a little splash.

Theseus turned back and couldn't believe his eyes. Ariadne had disappeared. In a flash he'd torn off his shirt and rushed to the side, sure she must have fallen in and was now waiting for him to rescue her in his strong arms.

But not at all. Instead, he saw his future wife confidently swimming through the water – long, powerful strokes – each one taking her farther away from him and nearer the island.

'What are you doing?' he shouted. 'Come back!'

But Ariadne took no notice. She was out of the sea now and walking up the sand.

'You can't go off on your own!' yelled Theseus. 'You're completely unprotected. Here – take this!' and waved his short stubby sword round and round his head.

But Ariadne just kept walking towards the trees. Finally, the moment before she disappeared into the forest, she turned and waved goodbye. Then, just like that, she was gone.

Theseus stood there frowning, his sword's ruby handle glinting in the sun, his mind completely befuddled. And he would never be any the wiser. Was she torn to pieces by ravenous wolves in the outskirts of the forest? Did she marry the flute player and start an orchestra? Maybe she learnt the magic of the island and became the High Priestess. Theseus would never know. Because he never saw her again.

Meanwhile back in the Kingdom of Minos, Daedalus and Icarus were imprisoned in a dark tower that was covered with ivy and surrounded by six muscular guards with faces as ugly as rotten tomatoes that someone's just stood on. Icarus was let out to work each day on the prison farm while his father stayed locked in alone, hunched over his work bench, making a new monster for Minos, a robot one that could never be beaten. But every moment he was racking his brains thinking how to escape.

Then one day, the shadow of a bird flew past, and Ping! it gave Daedalus an idea. And, of course, since he was Daedalus, it was a dead clever idea – when Daedalus' brain went 'Ping!', it was a ping worth listening to.

From now on, each evening Icarus smuggled feathers in his trousers from the farm's dovecote and wax from the farm's beehives. The guards used to laugh at the size of his bottom, stuffed full of stuff as it was, but Icarus didn't mind. He knew he'd have the last laugh. And every night, father and son worked on their means of escape. At first it looked like they were making a tiny model of a bird's wing. But then the model grew. And grew. After a couple of weeks they had made a huge wing, like the wing of a giant, swooping eagle. Then they made a second one, then a third, until hidden under their beds were two giant pairs of wings. They were going to fly to freedom.

At last the great day arrived. They waited impatiently for the sun to drop beneath the horizon, then strapped the massive wings tightly to their arms and shoulders and crawled out of the window of their cell on to the tiny ledge outside. It looked like a mile down to the bottom of the tower, and every gust of wind threatened to blow them off and send them crashing on to the rocks below.

'I do hope my calculations were correct,' said Daedalus nervously.

'You've never been wrong before, Dad,' replied Icarus.

'No, I suppose I haven't,' agreed his father and jumped off the ledge.

WHOOOSH!!!

Down he dropped like a stone, spiralling towards the cruel rocks below. Icarus shut his eyes in horror . . . and missed the most incredible sight in the world. Daedalus began to wave his arms about, the wings started to flap, and suddenly his downward plummet came to a halt and he rose up gently into the air again. Soon he was level with his son.

'You can open your eyes now,' he said. 'Come and join me.'

Icarus blinked in amazement. His Dad looked like a giant seagull with a very small beak.

'Hang on a second,' he replied. Then he squeezed back into the cell, grabbed the half completed monster his father had been working on, forced it out of the window, and KERBLANG! It smashed down right on

the heads of the tomato-faced guards. They crashed
to the ground, dazed and confused, and assumed it was
some kind of dream when, in the bright moonlight,
they looked up and
saw two human-shaped
birds fly away from
the tower and head
off towards Athens.

Soon Daedalus
and Son, Inventors
of Flying Machines
Extraordinary, had left
Minos' kingdom far behind
them and were speeding through the air
like a pair of fighter planes. All through
the night they flew until dawn broke.
'Don't fly too close to the sun,' called
Daedalus, 'or the wax will melt!'
But Icarus just laughed. He was
doing what no man had ever done
before – he was flying. It was
wonderful – he felt like a god.

He flew in loops.

In spirals.

Upside down.

Downside up.

He flew with one arm by his side and went round in circles. Then he flew with both arms by his side in a very

amusing imitation, jiggity-jig, of an extremely drunk sparrow.

'Don't fly too close to the sun!!' his father yelled again, 'OR THE WAX WILL MELT!!!'

But up and up went Icarus, higher and higher.

Only now there was something running down his body, down his legs and dripping into the sea – not that he noticed it.

He should have done.

It was melting wax.

And there were little white flurries like snow or tiny clouds – but he hardly noticed them either.

That was a mistake too.

They were doves' feathers.

And then he wasn't climbing any more, he was falling.

Down.

Down.

Down.

Down.

Until, with a tiny *splosh!* he dropped into the sea.

For hours Daedalus flew across the waves searching for Icarus. But he found nothing except a few wet feathers bobbing up and down on the surface of the quiet water.

Eventually, broken hearted, he left his son to his watery grave and flew sadly away. Only he wasn't heading for Athens now. He was flying away as far as he could, away from the Greeks, away from King Minos and away from all his memories . . . forever.

On board ship Theseus had been in a bad mood for days. Why had Ariadne left him like that? What was it she had wanted that he couldn't give her? After all, he was a pretty decent bloke really. And he had a fantastically muscly chest. Women were so illogical.

He chewed on a peanut and stared out to sea. Far away, a bird dropped out of the sky and plunged into the water.

What's it all about? thought Theseus. He didn't know. Then suddenly, the moment came that they had all been waiting and praying for.

'Land ho!' shouted the boy in the crow's nest. They rushed to the side of the boat, and, yes, there, far away on the horizon, sparkling like a jewel, was Athens. The fourteen young Athenians hugged each other and cried and cheered and danced all round the deck. Even the boy in the crow's nest had a little dance with a crow. They were home.

The boat moved gracefully and proudly, its black sails

billowing in the gentle wind, towards the white cliffs of Athens. At one point, if Theseus had been watching, he might have seen another figure dropping to his death – a man jumping off a cliff and smashing lifeless into the shingle. But Theseus wasn't looking. He was home, he was safe and the celebrations could begin. The ship glided alongside the pier, and Theseus leapt ashore, waiting for the medals, the brass bands, the cascades of flowers.

But where he had expected happiness, there was only sorrow . . .

'Your father King Aegeus is alive no longer,' said his heartbroken old nurse. 'He threw himself off the High Cliff when he saw your boat.'

'Why?' asked Theseus incredulously.

'He saw the black sails and thought you were dead. You forgot to change the sails to white.'

Theseus cried for a long time – deep racking sobs of guilt and sorrow. He couldn't make any sense of things. Then a thought struck him.

He looked up, wiped the tears from his eyes and said, 'That means I'm King, doesn't it?'

Back on his island, Minos lifted up the smashed remains of his mechanical Minotaur and hurled them into the sea. He was shaking with fury. Daedalus had tricked him twice. First he'd shown Theseus how to kill the Minotaur – and now he'd escaped from prison. Wherever he was hiding, Minos would find him, and when he found him, he would kill him . . . very slowly.

He picked up something from the seashore and gave his fawning courtiers a crooked smile. He had an idea. And King Minos loved his own ideas.

'I shall hold a competition,' he announced, 'open to anyone in the whole world. You see this tiny seashell, so small that you have to squint to get a good look at it? You see how it spirals round and round like a maze?'

The courtiers put on their glasses and clustered round.

'The first person cunning enough to pass a thread through every spiral of this shell shall win a fabulous prize – a life size bull of solid gold, with diamonds for eyes.'

'But who could perform such an impossible task, oh wise and magnificent Lord?' asked a particularly creepy courtier.

'Only one man in the world,' replied Minos. 'Our friend the maze maker. When the prize has been won, I'll have found Daedalus.' And then he laughed. The nastiest, cruellest laugh you ever heard.

*   *   *

At that moment Daedalus was carrying a lavatory into the palace of the King of Sicily. He put it down among a clutter of shower curtains and taps and bathroom suites, and began to route a pipe towards the guest bedroom.

The Sicilians were an easy going bunch. They slept a lot, danced a lot, and they didn't have regular meal times or inside plumbing. If they wanted a shower they'd use a waterfall, if they wanted a bath they'd lie in the sea. But the King didn't want to appear old-fashioned so, when Daedalus had appeared in Sicily alone and un-smiling, he'd been invited to install running water at the palace.

As Daedalus screwed on another section of plumbing, a jewelled crown popped up from behind an up-turned bath and the King said, 'I hope I'm not interrupting, but do you remember me asking you yesterday if you could pass a thread through the spirals of that shell I gave you?'

'Er . . . Yes,' said Daedalus vaguely, as he lay on his back behind a wash basin, fiddling away at a U-bend. Then he reached into his back pocket and passed something to the King. 'Here it is.'

Greedily the King snatched it and peered at it through an ivory magnifying glass. Sure enough, there was a tiny silk thread through every one of the shell's spirals. 'Brilliant!' exclaimed the King. 'How on earth did you do it?'

'Oh, it wasn't much of a problem,' replied Daedalus. 'I trained an ant to come when I called it, then tied the thread to its back leg, pushed it into the shell and kept on calling it until it crawled round and round and came out the other end. Pass me that adjustable spanner, would you?' he said and went on with his pipe laying.

The King rushed out of the room and began drafting a letter claiming his prize.

Within days Minos had arrived.

'Congratulations,' he said to the Sicilian King as he presented him with the golden bull. 'Tell me, did you solve the problem single handed?'

'Yes,' replied the King, 'virtually . . . Well, I mean, I had a little help from my plumber.'

'Your plumber!' hissed Minos and one corner of his mouth began to twitch. 'May I meet him?'

'Certainly,' replied the King magnanimously. 'Tonight we'll hold a celebration banquet and I shall invite him. In the meantime perhaps you'd like a bath. I've got a superb new guest bedroom with plenty of modern hot and cold water.'

Behind the King a curtain moved. It was as though someone had been listening.

Early that evening Minos lay in his bath smiling. Very soon he'd see Daedalus again and then the fun would begin. He smiled and slowly squeezed his bar of soap until it looked like porridge.

At that moment a trickle of hot water began to run out of the hot tap. 'Typical shoddy Sicilian workmanship!' thought Minos and leaned forward to turn it off – but the tap came away in his hands. Then hot water began running out of the cold tap – a second later Minos found himself with two taps in his hands. And now the water was getting hotter and hotter and the bathroom was filling with steam. In panic Minos tried to get out of the bath – but it was no use – now there was water pouring down from the ceiling. Scalding hot water. And a second later there was water shooting out of the walls – burning hot water.

Minos gave a scream of terror and fear – a scream that

sounded like a bull in a slaughterhouse, or the death agonies of the Minotaur. He clambered to his feet in blind panic, then he slipped on the porridgy soap and crashed back into the bath.

There was a hissing sound. Then silence. Minos lay under the bath water – dead clean and dead dead.

In the next room, Daedalus slowly turned a stop-cock and the water stopped. For the first time in months he gave a little smile. 'That's for my son Icarus,' he said.

4

The Trip to the Very Mouth of Hell

A blood curdling roar filled the air as the Athenians bore down on the rebels in a final charge. Armour thudded against armour, horses pawed the air in panic, and in the centre of it all was young King Theseus, his short stubby sword stained deep red. But suddenly, over towards the forest he saw a figure grab a loose horse and furtively slip away from the fighting. It was someone he knew all too well – his treacherous uncle Laius, sneaking away from the battle once again. But this time, he wasn't going to get away with it.

With one bound Theseus had mounted his white stallion, hacked his way through the seething crowd and set off in hot pursuit. A slow smile spread across his face – soon his final victory would be complete. He'd been King for two years now and Athens was so strong that no outsider dared attack it. Once Laius' lackies had been defeated nothing could stand in the way of Athens' greatness.

Theseus rode straight into the forest, his eyes flashing from side to side in search of his foe. He saw nothing, but heard a sound, so plunged on deeper and deeper into the undergrowth, like a dog following a fox's scent.

The sky grew darker above him, the air grew cold and wet, but still he pushed on after his evil uncle. Then suddenly, the scent went cold – and Theseus looked up to realise he was completely lost. Lost in the deepest, darkest corner of the forest.

He moved on aimlessly, hour after hour, rained on and exhausted, until he felt so weary he could barely keep his eyes open. But then, at last, when he was losing hope of ever finding a way out, he saw a faint glimmer of light. There ahead of him was an inn. A pretty gloomy old inn, but nevertheless somewhere he could rest until morning.

A door creaked slowly open and there stood a smiling sleek-faced man with skin the colour of a white rat.

'Do you have a spare bed?' asked the weary Theseus.

'Do I have a spare bed?' echoed the innkeeper, his high pitched voice quivering with excitement. 'I have the perfect bed for you, my dear.'

'Thanks,' replied Theseus gratefully. 'I'm dead tired.'

'Yes, I'm sure you are,' said the innkeeper and cackled wildly at some unexplained joke as he showed the young King to his room.

He's mad, thought Theseus, *but what do I care?*

He slumped on to the bed and blew out the light. The room was in total darkness.

Half an hour later the door slowly opened again. There stood the innkeeper, a candle in his shaky hand. Another man stood behind him. Flickering candle light played across his face – it was uncle Laius.

'Look at his legs, my Lord. They're too long,' hissed the innkeeper, pointing at Theseus' boots sticking out the end of the bed.

'I'm sure you can remedy that,' came the soft reply.

The innkeeper giggled insanely and drew out a meat cleaver.

'Dead tired, eh?' he whispered. Then, 'Tired and Dead, more likely!' he screamed, raised the cleaver in the air and struck.

Flum! Flum! The blade cut through Theseus' boots like butter.

Laius let out a tiny screech of joy, then froze as he felt the point of a knife pressing against his back. He turned and saw Theseus with a pleasant smile on his face. He'd been standing behind the door. The boots in the bed belonged to him all right, but they were as empty as a pair of coconuts.

'If I'd been younger,' Theseus said, 'I'd have killed you straight away. Unfortunately I can no longer afford to give myself that pleasure. Instead I'm going to put you on trial. When the Athenians hear my story, and realise how foul and depraved you and your followers are, they'll exile you for ever,' and he trussed the two wretches up like chickens, flung them over his horse, and slowly rode back to Athens.

But when he reached the city it was in uproar. Shop-keepers were nailing up their windows, carts were being rolled over and turned into make-shift barricades, half-mad people were rushing in all directions, clutching bundles of possessions. Everywhere there were dogs barking, cats miaowing and pigs oinking their tails off; all their masters had scarpered in the mad rush.

A terrified butcher was hurtling down the road wearing a necklace of sausages and carrying a cage full of chickens and a cash register. Theseus leant out of his saddle and grabbed him by a giblet.

'What's the matter?'

'It's the pirates, my Lord,' came the terrified reply. 'They've landed at Marathon and they're coming this way!'

Theseus drew a deep breath. Being King wasn't exactly restful.

Then he galloped to the Palace, rode up the Palace steps (only he was allowed to do that), and let out an almighty yell: 'HARRROOOO!!!'

It was a secret sign: within ten seconds, a dozen of his best men sat mounted before him at attention on a dozen of his best horses.

'Trouble,' said Theseus. And they set off to face it.

An hour later, they arrived, breathless, at the flat grassy plain of Marathon. In front of them, armed to their

72

rotting teeth and grinning like mad monkeys were fifty mean pirates – and they hadn't come to picnic. The two small armies faced each other. Most of the Athenians wore golden belts, most of the pirates had one eye. Most of the Athenians were clean shaven, most of the pirates had beards so rough you could have used them for scrubbing really dirty frying pans. There was silence. You could have heard a pin drop. In fact one did drop out of the nose of one of the pirates, and everyone heard it.

Then a figure stepped out of the pirate ranks. He was a huge black man, with a mass of hair which dangled down the side of his body in a plait, a ruby ear-ring, gold teeth and a scar which ran from the corner of his grinning mouth right up to where his ear lobe would have been if it hadn't been chopped off in a fight. But most of all, he was tall: he looked like he'd been stretched and stayed that way.

'I've heard tell of an Athenian King named Theseus,' he drawled, and his voice rumbled like thunder across the water. 'I've heard he's brave and fearless and that he killled the Cretan monster. Which one is he?'

Theseus stepped forward and gave a tiny nod.

'Then I, Pirithous, King of the Pirates, challenge you to single combat.'

Theseus gave another little nod – this time accompanied by a tiny smile. To be honest, this sort of thing was rather his cup of tea. He'd never cared for the quiet life.

In an instant, the two armies had formed a circle round Theseus and the giant Pirate King. The two heroes stood motionless, their hands poised just above their sword hilts. Deeply they gazed into each others' eyes, each one knowing that if he lost concentration even for a second, it would mean instant death and his head rolling around on the ground like a big potato.

Hour upon hour went by. Neither man so much as twitched. The two armies were tense and motionless.

Then, towards evening, a lark rose out of the grass, higher and higher it flew, singing its little heart out; for one fateful instant Pirithous' eyes flickered and . . . SHONK! Theseus struck.

In a blur and a spin, Pirithous' sword flew into the air –

In a sudden jolt his legs were kicked from underneath him –

In a flash of a fist his nose was punched into his head –

And there stood Theseus, his sword above his head, ready to deliver the fatal blow.

Pirithous lay on the grass smiling ruefully.

'I've lost,' he said. 'Still, that bird was singing a real pretty song. Look – the soldiers must be getting a bit peckish. Take my life now, will you, so they can go get something to eat.'

Theseus looked him up and down, and just couldn't help smiling. 'No,' he said. 'I won't take your life. I'll take your friendship. Here, let me give you a hand.' And reaching down, he pulled Pirithous to his feet.

Everyone cheered and Pirithous and Theseus swore eternal friendship, there on the Plain of Marathon. The Pirates and the Athenians cuddled each other and swapped belts and eye-patches, and soon they were all riding back to Athens surrounded by happy townspeople. Peanut-sellers and patch-salesmen were out in force and the terrified butcher made a fortune out of grilled sausages.

Next morning Laius and the mad innkeeper were put on trial and were banished for life to an uninhabited island – with only each other's foul presence for company. At last Athens was completely safe. There were no wars, no riots, no street fighting – it was a place where everyone wanted to be. Theseus' old friend and teacher Hercules came to stay (when he wasn't too busy slaughtering man-eating donkeys or biting the heads off seven-headed monsters), and his other old teacher Daedalus was a permanent guest, forever designing new wonders for the city.

There was no Minotaur, no rebellion, no fear – which meant . . .

Theseus was bored! The city was full of artists – but one statue looked pretty much like the next to him; and it was full of actors – but he always fell asleep during their plays. What Theseus wanted was a good old punch-up – just like in the old days.

Then one day he caught Pirithous gazing moodily out of the window staring at the sea.

'What's up?' he asked.

'I'm in love,' came the reply.

Theseus started to laugh. He roared, he guffawed, he rolled around on the floor hooting with derision.

'In love! You!' he said finally wiping the tears from his eyes. 'You great soft wimp! Who is she?'

'I've only seen her once,' replied his moonstruck friend. 'Her name's Persephone and she's the Queen of the Underworld. Do you think she'd come away with me if I asked her?'

'Bound to,' said Theseus. 'She'd be crazy not to. You're a really regular guy.'

Then there was a long pause as they both stared at the grey ocean. Finally Theseus spoke again. And now his eyes were shining with excitement.

'I know,' he said. 'Let's go get her. We'll take your pirate ship and sail on until we actually reach the entrance to the Underworld.' This was the adventure he'd been waiting for – the greatest adventure of them all. The trip to the very mouth of Hell.

No one ever said it would be easy. Through tempests they sailed, through whirlwinds, through seas so clotted with seaweed that the oars snapped like match sticks when the sailors leant on them. Then, finally, just when they thought they were clear, a massive mauve sea monster rose from the ocean depths and bit the boat in two. Water poured into its severed halves and the ship and its crew sank slowly to a watery grave.

Only Pirithous and Theseus had the brains to climb to the top of the mast and vault on to the creature's back. It shook itself, it twisted, it dived, it jumped and it roared with irritation as it tried to shake them off; but they clung to its slippery stinking scales for dear life.

Finally, exhausted, the monster heaved itself up on to a desolate beach, collapsed, and fell fast asleep. And the two exhausted sailors fell asleep too in the folds of its skin.

Next morning they awoke to the deafening sound of the creature snoring. They slipped off its back, patted it on the nose and watched as it dozily crawled down to the water's edge and swam off.

It was only now that they bothered to turn and see where they were. It certainly wasn't home. In fact, it was more like . . . Hell.

It was bleak. Very bleak. There was no life, no vegetation, and certainly no fast-food: just choking grey smoke, black cliffs, dribbles of molten lava, and high above them a dark, threatening volcano puffing poisonous green smoke out of its twin craters.

'It's no holiday camp, is it?' murmured Theseus gloomily, but Pirithous was smiling.

'Who'd have thought it?' he said. 'Who ever would

have thought it? This is the place we've been looking for. All we have to do is find a way to get inside that volcano and we'll be at the entrance to the Underworld!'

And so, all alone, the two heroes set off to raid the Underworld. For days they picked their way across the scorching landscape, searching for a cave which would lead them to the Kingdom of Persephone. Then at last Theseus said, 'OW!!' and their problems were solved. He had stubbed his toe on a tiny crack in the smooth side of the mountain. Theseus slipped his fingers in, and then clenched his fist. The crack became a fissure. Then they both forced their arms in, and heaved, so the fissure became a hole: then they pushed and they shoved and they squeezed in their whole bodies, and then wriggled until . . .

Suddenly, phwoosh!!!!, they were inside the volcano . . .

As the hole closed slowly behind them, they could see they were standing in a cave the size of a cathedral. There were silver stalagmites going upwards, golden stalactites coming downwards, and the walls and ceiling were encrusted with diamonds. At the far end was a dark tunnel. When they reached it they drew their swords and stepped firmly into the darkness. One step, two steps, three steps forward and then VOOOOM!! the ground disappeared from under them and their legs flayed about in the empty air as they went.

Down

Down

Down

Down

tumbling head over heels until WHACK! they landed in a heap on a black shining floor.

Then they heard a laugh – a soft purring laugh that was so strange it made their stomachs feel funny – like they'd just swallowed something furry. Bruised and puzzled they looked up.

Ahead of them, on a throne of glistening black coal sat the woman they had been searching for – Queen Persephone. She was tall, she was beautiful, and she was stroking two giant moles which lay snuggled in her lap.

'Sorry to burst in on you like this,' said Pirithous cheerfully, 'but I love you and want you to come away with me.'

One of the moles started mewing. 'And what if I don't wish to come, big boy?' replied Persephone.

'Then we'll carry you off with us,' said Theseus, chuckling.

'Some people never learn,' murmured Persephone to her big brown pets.

Then she snapped her fingers. Out of nowhere an enormous sofa appeared. It was most certainly not the kind of thing you see in the average sitting room. Instead of little flowers, it had huge creeping plants embroidered on it, and its legs were carved in the shape of giant writhing snakes. Nevertheless, when Persephone gestured towards it, Pirithous and Theseus politely sat down.

That was a big mistake. Because this was no ordinary sofa. ZOOOONK!!! Immediately the carved snakes came to life and wound themselves round their legs and arms. The creeping plants burst into flower and wrapped their tendrils around the bodies of the two heroes. Then the cushions melted into sticky holdfast glue and they couldn't move an inch. If you've ever felt stuck on a sofa talking to someone boring, it was nothing compared to this. These guys were never going to get out.

'Help!!!' they yelled. 'Let us out!'

At least that's what they tried to yell, but they couldn't. When they opened their mouths not a sound came out – which is no surprise. A big snake had

wrapped itself round their faces, from ear to ear.

'You will remain here for ever,' said Persephone, 'silent and stupid. You men – with your noise and your boasting and silly little pointed swords. Me – come away with *you*? I'd rather run away with an unattractive hippopotamus.'

And having put them firmly in their place, she politely disappeared into thin air.

It was not a good situation. For weeks the friends sat glued to their sofa, and the harder they wriggled, the tighter they were trapped. They couldn't eat or drink because the stupid snake had fallen asleep on their faces. Soon they both looked like skeletons – half-dead dead men in the land of the dead. Theseus, the King who killed the Minotaur, had a feeling his luck had run out.

But then, one day, they woke to the sound of a terrifying hammering on the ceiling above. Boom. Boom. Boom!!

Then BOOOOMMM!!!!

The ceiling cracked open and daylight flooded in. Seconds later, a rope snaked down to the ground, followed by a big burly man. The biggest burliest man in the world. Yes – it was Hercules. And not a moment too soon.

'I thought I might find you here,' he said and sprinted towards the sofa. And well he might – there was no time to spare. Straight away, Queen Persephone's voice echoed round the cavern.

'Who has dared enter the Underworld?' she
screamed.

In a flash, the walls began to shake, boulders crashed
down from the ceiling and the floor started to crack,
leaving huge gaping holes that bubbled slimy purple
lava. Hercules had to move fast. He dodged and weaved
as trickily as an Argentinian footballer until he made it

85

to the sofa with only a couple of flesh wounds. Once there, he wrapped his strong arms round his old pupil Theseus and the veins stood out on his bronzed biceps like veins on a piece of marble as he pulled and pulled to free him from the Sofa of Death.

ZERRROINCH!! There was a long tearing noise like the sound of a giant zip being opened and in a flash Theseus was free. He would have run off straight away, but there was such an agonising throbbing in his rear end that he had to take a look behind. It was not a pretty sight. Unfortunately, that ripping sound had been the sound of his bottom. Half of it was still left on the sofa.

(And for those of you who are interested in useless facts, that is why, to this day, Athenians have such small bottoms.)

But this was no time for gathering interesting facts. Hercules dragged his half-bottomed friend across the slippery black floor, avoiding rocks and lava and falling debris, until finally Theseus made it to the rope and began to inch his way back to daylight. Then Hercules remembered Pirithous and turned back to the sofa to get him. But it was too late. The whole floor now began groaning and writhing and bubbling – in fact it wasn't a floor at all, but a hideous hot purple lake. Slowly the sofa began to sink. Pirithous looked up at Theseus and they both knew this was goodbye. And as he disappeared into the lava for ever, Pirithous raised his arm above his head

in a silent farewell salute. Soon all
you could see was his hand.
Then only his fingers, then
only his fingernails, and
finally – nothing but a
black eye patch and a ruby
ear-ring floating on the bubbling waters.

Some time later, Theseus lay propped up on the deck of
Hercules' ship, swathed in bandages. The sky was full
of jet black smoke, lit only by the inferno from which
he'd just escaped.

He looked up at Hercules. 'Thanks,' he said huskily.

'You've found your voice then.'

'Yes,' replied King Theseus quietly. 'But I've lost
the best friend I ever had.' And as he sailed back towards
home, far below in the bowels of the earth, Persephone
prowled her lonely corridors with her blind moles in her
arms and smiled at the revenge she'd wreaked on the
puny men who dared invade her kingdom. She was sorry
to lose the sofa, but hell, she thought, everything costs
you something.

Back in Athens the boys received a hero's welcome.

'Theseus has returned from the Underworld,'
everyone cried. 'Long live Theseus! Theseus the hero!
Theseus the immortal! Theseus the God!'

But Theseus had lost his friend, his ship, and half his

bottom – and his dreams were haunted by the look of contempt in Persephone's eyes. He felt a total failure.

After that, years went by and Athens grew bigger and more powerful. Soon it was the centre of the whole known world. But its famous King hardly spoke to anyone. All he ever seemed to do was stare out at the sea, as he slowly turned into an old man.

Then one spring morning, there was a knock at the palace door. Standing there was a proud young man looking just like Theseus had twenty years before.

'My Lord,' he said. 'My name is Jason. I'm sailing to the far away land of Colchis to steal the Golden Fleece. I've got room for twenty heroes. You may be old, but you're top of my list. How about it?'

Theseus didn't say a word. He kicked off his velvet slippers and pulled on his old sandals; he slipped out of his dressing gown and slapped on some oil; he threw away his crown and strapped on his short stubby sword; then he put his arm around Jason's shoulder and the two of them walked out of the palace without once looking back.

Bobbing gently in the harbour was Jason's golden boat. Theseus climbed aboard and took his place. On one side of him sat Hercules picking his teeth. On the other sat Daedalus making a compass from the bones of a dolphin. At last Theseus was really home. Home on the open sea, in search of adventure.

Jason gave the word and the twenty heroes leant on their oars. Out of the harbour they rowed, across the wide ocean and over the horizon towards Colchis. If they'd known what horrors were in store they might not have gone . . .

But that's another story.

ABOUT THE AUTHORS

Tony Robinson plays Baldrick in the television series, Black Adder and presents and co-produces Channel 4's archaeology series, Time Team. He wrote four series of BBC TV's Maid Marian and Her Merry Men in which he also played the Sheriff of Nottingham. He has written sixteen children's books and has won numerous awards as a writer of children's television programmes, including two Royal Television Society awards, a BAFTA, and the International Prix Jeunesse. He has appeared in over one thousand television programmes but enjoys staying in his Bristol home, writing.

Richard Curtis began writing comedy after leaving Oxford University in 1978. He has written for, amongst others, Not the Nine O'Clock News, Black Adder, Mr Bean, The Vicar of Dibley, and Comic Relief, which he co-founded and co-produces for the BBC. He has also written two films, The Tall Guy and Four Weddings And A Funeral, for which he won the Writers Guild Awards in America and the UK and the Evening Standard, Comedy and London Critics Awards. In order to prepare for this book he studied Classics at Papplewick and Harrow School, and Greek at Oxford. He was made an MBE in 1994, and lives in Notting Hill with his partner, Emma Freud, and their daughter, Scarlett.

ODYSSEUS, SUPERHERO

Tony Robinson and Richard Curtis

The moment he met her, Odysseus knew Helen was trouble! Now she's been kidnapped and he's promised to get her back. Ships set sail, swords are sharpened and sights are set on Troy. Years of fighting lie ahead – bloody battles and fearful deaths . . . But Odysseus has a secret weapon – in the shape of a wooden horse . . .

ODYSSEUS, GOES THROUGH HELL

Tony Robinson and Richard Curtis

Odysseus hasn't seen his wife for years – now, at last, he's on his way home from Troy.

But it seems his adventures are far from over . . .

First he must outwit the one-eyed Cyclops and escape from the enchantress Circe, be guided by ghosts through the Land of the Dead and ignore the sweet sounds of the deadly sirens . . .

Will Odysseus make it home alive?

WHAT THEY DON'T TELL YOU ABOUT ANCIENT EGYPTIANS

David Jay

Did you know that teething babies were given fried mice to chew on?
Or that policemen used monkeys to arrest people?
And did you know that the world's first recorded strike was held by pyramid builders?

The Ancient Egyptians lived half of their lives up to their eyes in mud, the other half choking on desert sand, and spent most of their time thinking about dying! Any history book will give you the boring facts THEY think you should know, but only this one will tell you just how weird life in Ancient Egypt REALLY was . . .

WHAT THEY DON'T TELL YOU ABOUT VILLAINS THROUGH THE AGES

Jim Hatfield

Did you know that King Mithridates trained himself to drink poison?
Or that Adolf Hitler was a vegetarian?
And did you know that the most villainous Roman of all, Caligula, made his horse a member of the government?

From small time crooks to big-time barbarians, all the gory details you ever wanted to know about the dregs of humanity are right here. Any history book will give you the boring facts THEY think you should know about the bad guys, but only this one REALLY scrapes the bottom of the barrel . . .

ORDER FORM

0 340 66497 5	Odysseus, Superhero *Tony Robinson & Richard Curtis*	£3.99
0340 664983	Odysseus Goes Through Hell *Tony Robinson & Richard Curtis*	£3.99
0340 65614 X	What They Don't Tell You About Ancient Egyptians *David Jay*	£3.50
0 340 63624 6	What They Don't Tell You About Villains Through The Ages *Jim Hatfield*	£3.50
0 340 65613 1	What They Don't Tell You About Elizabeth I *Bob Fowke*	£3.50

All Hodder Children's books are available at your local bookshop or newsagent, or can be ordered direct from the publisher. Just tick the titles you want and fill in the form below. Prices and availability subject to change without notice.

Hodder Children's Books, Cash Sales Department, Bookpoint, 39 Milton Park, Abingdon, OXON, OX14 4TD, UK. If you have a credit card you may order by telephone – (01235) 831700.

Please enclose a cheque or postal order made payable to Bookpoint Ltd to the value of the cover price and allow the following for postage and packing:
UK & BFPO – £1.00 for the first book, 50p for the second book, and 30p for each additional book ordered up to a maximum charge of £3.00.
OVERSEAS & EIRE – £2.00 for the first book, £1.00 for the second book, and 50p for each additional book.

Name ....

Address ....

....

If you would prefer to pay by credit card, please complete:
Please debit my Visa/Access/Diner's Card/American Express (delete as applicable) card no:

Signature ....

Expiry Date ....